Catching the Moon

MYLA GOLDBERG

pictures by CHRIS SHEBAN

story by Myla Goldberg and David Gassaway

ARTHUR A. LEVINE BOOKS AN IMPRINT OF SCHOLASTIC INC.

Hardly anyone noticed when the Fisherwoman started fishing at night.

In the morning, she would be so worn out that she could barely bait her hook. The fishermen figured she was growing old.

Night followed night, and the Man in the Moon began to worry.

"She must be getting terribly hungry, fishing like that!" he fretted.

As she sat beneath the moon-bright sky, the
Fisherwoman felt a tug on her line.

"Skunk feathers!" she grumbled when she saw
what she had caught. "If it was crustacean I was after,
I'd be out in a boat and not perched here like some
fool nightcrawler." But that didn't stop her from
cooking up a steaming pot of lobster stew.

Now everyone knows that on one night each month, there is no moon: From Iowa to India, the sky is dark, save for its starlight freckles.

On those nights, the Fisherwoman stayed in her shack and brewed green tea — and the Man in the Moon put on his traveling hat.

She was not one for entertaining guests.

"What is it?" she grumbled to the round-faced man who appeared at her door.

"Sea cucumber sandwich?" he gleamed in reply.

She didn't plan to let him in; she didn't expect to nibble his sandwiches; and she certainly didn't suppose she'd find them so delicious.

As it happened, she and her visitor shared a fondness for tea.

"Why is your house so full of holes?" he asked as the tide rushed in to soak the floor.

"Who on earth wears nighttime sunglasses?" she answered.

Just then, a wave came crashing through the door, soaking their shoes, upsetting the table, and knocking the kettle and cups to the floor.

"My tea!" cried the Fisherwoman.

"My heavens!" cried her guest. "I'm afraid I've caused a mess!"

Even the tide could not erase the trail of luminous footprints her visitor left behind.

A month passed.

By night, the Fisherwoman cast her line into the moon's reflection, reeling in a new kettle and two china teacups and grumbling all the while. By day, the fishermen shook their heads, sure she'd become old and sea-addled.

The Fisherwoman paid them no mind.

On the next month's moonless night, the Fisherwoman was brewing black tea when there was a knock at her door.

"What is it?" she asked, peering through the luminous keyhole.

"Moon pie?" came the shining reply.

Through mouths sticky with marshmallow, they talked of seaweed and sailfish, currents and carp.

"Any luck fishing?" asked her guest, but the Fisherwoman shook her head. "Have you tried trading your mouse for a worm?" he offered.

"A worm?" The Fisherwoman tittered. "A worm?" She shrieked and guffawed. Her shoulders shook, her chin quivered, and she almost fell out of her chair. "What use is a worm for the likes of the moon, who is made out of nothing but cheese?"

"You mean," gasped her guest, who turned paler still, "that you aren't angling for fish?"

And so she confessed what no one had guessed: She spoke of the troublesome tide. Every day it nibbled the piers and shacks, carrying bits and bites back out to sea.

"High tide is a greedygut!" she cried. "It won't stop gobbling until our shacks and our piers are nothing but wormy old driftwood!"

The Fisherwoman knew that the moon controlled the tides.

"With my trusty mouse and his nose for cheese, I'm sure to hook the Man in the Moon. And once I do, I won't throw him back until he's agreed to keep high tide away!"

Her bright-eyed guest was very impressed, but
he did not share her fondness for fishing hooks.
   The Fisherwoman thought his face looked awfully
familiar.

Another month passed with not a nibble from the moon, but the Fisherwoman did catch some very peculiar paint. For the first time, she whistled as she walked down her dock, her catch *clang-a-clanging* at her side.

The next night, rather than fish by moonlight, the Fisherwoman painted her shack. "Moonbeam, moonbeam, keeping away the tide," she sang as her walls took on a familiar glow.

"Thank you!" she called up to the Man in the Moon, but of course, he couldn't hear her.

The next moonless night, the Fisherwoman
opened her door before her friend had even
docked his boat.

"Yellow tea?" she asked with a smile.

"I've brought the coral honey," he beamed.

Perhaps the honey combined with the calm of the sea; or maybe it was the kettle and the wash of warm voices, but that night's tea was the best they'd ever tasted.

Since that grand, moonless night, turtle babies have grown up to lay eggs of their own, dolphins have swum to Bali and back, and hermit crabs have shed their shells too many times to count. Generations of salmon have swum upstream, sharks have lost and regrown clutches of teeth, and an amazing thing has happened: High tide has been kept away for so long that the fishing shacks now claim an island of their own.

Their soft glow makes the sky seem a little less big and the earth seem a little less small.

"Hello!" the Fisherwoman calls to the moon each night that he's in the sky.

Maybe he can hear her after all.

For Zelie — M.G.

For my mom — C.S.

Text copyright © 2007 by Myla Goldberg • Illustrations copyright © 2007 by Chris Sheban • All rights reserved. Published by Arthur A. Levine Books, an imprint of Scholastic Inc., *Publishers since 1920.* SCHOLASTIC and the LANTERN LOGO are trademarks and/or registered trademarks of Scholastic Inc. No part of this publication may be reproduced, stored in a retrieval system, or transmitted in any form or by any means, electronic, mechanical, photocopying, recording, or otherwise, without written permission of the publisher. For information regarding permission, write to Scholastic Inc., Attention: Permissions Department, 557 Broadway, New York, NY 10012. • Library of Congress Cataloging-in-Publication Data Goldberg, Myla. Catching the moon / by Myla Goldberg ; illustrated by Chris Sheban. p. cm. Summary: Using a mouse as bait instead of a worm, an old woman fishes all night long, confusing the fishermen as well as the Man in the Moon. ISBN-13: 978-0-439-57686-4 ISBN-10: 0-439-57686-5 [1. Moon—Fiction. 2. Fishing—Fiction.] I. Sheban, Chris, ill. II. Title. PZ7.G56438Cat 2007 [E]—dc22 2006013849 • 10 9 8 7 6 5 4 3 2 1 • 07 08 09 10 11 • First edition, May 2007 Printed in Singapore 46 • The art was created using watercolor and Prismacolor pencils on Arches paper • Book design by Richard Amari